"*Seeing People Off* is a fascinating novel. Fans of inward-looking postmodernists like Clarice Lispector will find much to admire here."
—NPR

"Stunning... [Beňová] has created that unique and uniquely satisfying phenomenon of a page-turner that must yet be read slowly and precisely."
—*Necessary Fiction*

"[Beňová] is in the first generation of post-Soviet writers for whom scarcity and censorship is a recent memory, and the political is always lurking just behind the breezy Aimee Bender–like prose."
—*Publishers Weekly*

"These stories explore death and other kinds of leaving in wry, fresh ways. The end of childhood, the end of an affair, the end of sanity—when I arrived at the end of this book, I found myself returning to the beginning. This is a merry-go-round one can hold on to."
—*Kenyon Review*

"Beňová's short, fast novels are a revolution against normality. Unlike so many others, her novels not only claim to be a revolution but actually achieve this feat through their minimalist narratives that go against all conventions; in fact, Beňová manages to subtly and intelligently poke fun at conventional categorizations."
—*Austrian Broadcasting Corporation, ORF*

Away! Away!

JANA BEŇOVÁ

Translated by Janet Livingstone

A Novel

Two Dollar Radio
Books too loud to Ignore

Two Dollar Radio
Books too loud to Ignore

WHO WE ARE TWO DOLLAR RADIO is a family-run outfit dedicated to reaffirming the cultural and artistic spirit of the publishing industry. We aim to do this by presenting bold works of literary merit, each book, individually and collectively, providing a sonic progression that we believe to be too loud to ignore.

TWODOLLARRADIO.com

Proudly based in
Columbus
OHIO

🐦 @TwoDollarRadio

📷 @TwoDollarRadio

f /TwoDollarRadio

Love the
PLANET?
So do we.

Printed on Rolland Enviro, which contains 100% post-consumer fiber, is ECOLOGO, Processed Chlorine Free, Ancient Forest Friendly and FSC® certified and is manufactured using renewable biogas energy.

PERMANENT   100%   BIO GAS ENERGY   Ancient Forest Friendly™

Printed in Canada

SOME RECOMMENDED LOCATIONS FOR READING *AWAY! AWAY!*:
Elevated places—tops of hills, vineyards. Cafés and wine bars with high spirits.
Double-decker buses, planes, hot air balloons, and trees.
Or, pretty much anywhere because books are portable and the perfect technology!

AUTHOR PHOTOGRAPH→
Vladimir Simicek

TRANSLATOR PHOTOGRAPH→
Janet Livingstone

IMAGE→
The Ladies' Home Journal (1889)

ANYTHING ELSE? Unfortunately, yes. Do not copy this book—with the exception of quotes used in critical essays and reviews—without the written permission of the publisher.
WE MUST ALSO POINT OUT THAT THIS IS A WORK OF *FICTION*. Names, characters, places, and incidents are products of the author's lively imagination. Any resemblance to real events or persons, living or dead, is entirely coincidental, with the exception of Gerda, Kai, and the reindeer from the fairytale *The Snow Queen* by Hans Christian Andersen.

THIS BOOK HAS RECEIVED A SUBSIDY FROM SLOLIA Committee,
the Centre for Information on Literature in Bratislava, Slovakia.

Away!

"*There was once a preserved restless stone in Kyzyl,
which served as an anchor for Argonauts.
It ran away so often they had to pour molten lead over it.*"

The boy named Son—like the common suffix on Nordic surnames—doesn't like strangers' homes or large groups of people. And what scares him most are large groups of people at strangers' homes. He lingers in the doorway and turns around, escaping through his parents' legs.

"Away! Away!" he says, pressing their knees apart.

Rosa is a child of the Main Station. Directly behind the fence of the house where she was born begins the Great Chinese Wall of the railroad. The cross-ties pulse, rails accelerate to a gallop. Regular collisions. All the couchettes in the sleeping car point north.

A Prague knight once wrote about his little sister. In childhood, they were brought up together in a German boarding school and visited Princess Thurn und Taxis. When she asked what they wished for, the little sister refused, saying it wasn't polite. Very rude. It begins with a 'W'.

The Princess insisted.

Little girl: Weg! Weg!

Rosa, a child of the Main Station, is forty years old. She crossed the tracks daily all those many years, first on her way to school and then to work. On her way to the city buses, she passed the trains. All manner of public transport and city roads begin beyond the tunnel. The trains sit on the platforms right behind her house. All you have to do is start running andddddd / jump.

Switch cities (like) masks.

Choose distance instead of access.

Roads and pubs.

Rosa. Downtown, there's a blinking display of the date, time and current temperature. Underneath it, my life grows subtly shorter. Flows away. The clock is a warning: a harvester of wasted days, months, degrees Celsius.

The foundation of a creative life is skipping out. Adventure. Rosa remembers that as a child she couldn't understand why kids skipped. She liked school, it was her first performance space, she had friends there. And she was attached to the teachers.

Her elementary school was in town, but for high school Rosa ended up on the outskirts—on the edge of town, in a depressing neighborhood with such big, wide transport arteries that a pedestrian never knew where to cross. It was a place for machines, cars and buses, covered in black snow and dust, no obstacles or residents to slow them down. No genuine life. Just speed. Wind. Away! Away! An empty, speechless landscape without nature, without people, without architecture. Completely different students, too. While it was mainly city children who went to the elementary school, this high school was full of kids from the Provinces.

The Provinces and Lapa. The worst neighborhood in the city.

Provincial children failed to see the difference between themselves and grown-ups. Upon graduating, Rosa's classmate, who is now a police detective, considered the biggest victory of her high school career to be smoking on school grounds in front of teachers. This didn't appeal to Rosa, who preferred to smoke alone in the evenings while strolling through the empty city. (Young lady, don't smoke while you walk on the street like some kind of slut, light up properly, inside a coffee shop, an older man said once, approaching her on the street.) The teachers were of the same generation as Rosa's parents, so she lumped them into the same group—patrician. If only because they were adults. It was too much for them. They needed respect. Protection.

The first few days of high school, she cried often. It particularly got to her in the cafeteria. Ever since she was a kid, she couldn't stand eating in a group. The spaces, sounds and smells of the cafeteria depressed her. Even after finishing class, you have to remain in your group to eat, rushed by the teachers, with just one meal choice, and no say over portion size. The oversight and discipline never stop. As she ate, she longed to be a free person, *a real human being*—not a student. She wanted to be part of the *big world*, not the collective.

Rosa. It was somewhere here that my yearning for independence began, after being so limited: instead of lunches in the school cafeteria, as a kid I started going to the department store for egg salad sandwiches and Coke. (Freedom & Anarchy!) There was a tiny little self-service snack bar there, right behind the toy department. There, all of us eaters were independent and grown up. Equality & brotherhood & freedom.

She began skipping in the second year of high school. In 1990. (If you know what I mean!)[1] After she met Son. They sat in a café every evening and talked. Laughed, mourned. She started smoking. High time to start, really—sixteen years old!

Rosa. I've *loved* red wine for some time now. After those evenings, it was impossible to go to school in the morning. You *couldn't* get on the bus and take off for the outskirts. Leaving the *city and yourself behind*. I remember how I bought, by myself at the station, three cigarettes and a glass of mulled wine, put on my Walkman and slowly, so that the wine didn't spill, walked toward town. The surface of the liquid, breath and gate in sync. The tree-lined alley to the Main Station, the crowns of the trees entangled with each other above my head, the cigarette smoke, the smell of cloves—in a word, Paris.

And in the mornings, I would pack my bag and leave the house at the usual time. Away! Away! I thought about how I used to stay home sick as a kid, how I was surprised at the house itself. It was suddenly different—without my brother and parents in the rooms, secret and scary—all there just for me.

My world at sixteen felt similar, my lack of freedom was confined to one space, and from eight o' clock on, it spun away from me. In my free time, I ran in the other direction with a light

---

1   At the end of 1989, the communist regime in Czechoslovakia fell.

step, to a place with no buses, only streetcar bells and the whirr of trolleybuses. Clutching the book I was reading, I walked through the streets of the old town, past the cafés. I read almost all of Kafka's *Castle* at the foot of Castle Hill. How pathetic... Like puberty.

Or Paris. You find it within yourself at sixteen years old—just like that, from one day to the next, especially at dusk—in your own city, or it's forever lost to you.

Then, it's forever wiped out from the world, sometime around eighteen years old, boom, it gets swallowed up by the Earth.

And you can say good-bye to it, erase it from your head forever.

The advantage was that she had *predictable* parents—she knew where they worked and what routes they took from home to work or to go shopping. Bratislava is a city with closed-off neighborhoods, like remote continents. In Lapa, Rosa doesn't meet anyone from her family or from work. In the old town, the same people have been circulating for years, slowly aging in the cafés of her childhood.

Rosa. Despite my sense of security, it was clear that eventually they would figure out I was skipping. But this only gave that time a certain cachet. The cachet of treasure. Stolen time that you should enjoy: *I definitely* started writing poetry.

Today, she almost didn't make it to work. Like it used to be in high school. She got up in the morning, left the house, but then just kept walking as she passed by that unpleasant building with her desk and the monitor in front of her face. Without blinking, she continued farther through the wintry city and wandered into a shop, where she put a bag of oranges, rolls, cheese and peppers in her basket—as if for an outing. A person with a history of crossing borders (into drugs, alcohol, food, lying, skipping out, unfaithfulness) easily backslides straight to the peak of their worst impulses—and their rock bottom. To the exposed nerve emitting heat. Like a moth/nightmare.

It's raining and snowing on and off and she feels like she's never felt such hüzün before. But it's not true, she had the same thing last January. Every January. Only a meeting with Klaus Chapter one winter revived her. The old writer was sitting in the middle of a café full of people, glowing. He was laughing, talking, eyes shining—a firecracker of energy. She felt as if he had thrown a coat or rain jacket over her—a blanket full of fireflies. Nothing ethereal, just a heavy, thick covering—or maybe actually a physical body. Of a strong old man. A body full of light, joy, energy. Babbling with life!

Rosa. My scratched-up head hurts, the wounds are throbbing. Yesterday I wrote to Son telling him that over my lunch breaks I escape from work at 1:00pm just as they're opening the night bar, and I drink. I knock down one margarita after another.

She discovered tequila.

One could say.

Like when the sculptor discovered a skull—he took it under his arm and didn't come out of his atelier for a year.

Rosa. I'm trapped. I want to lie in bed next to Son, but instead, I'm sitting at work, a cramp personified. A trapped, bare, blood-soaked winter bone.

Her head, exactly in the spots where her hair & unconsciousness begin, is scratched bloody. It's piling up under her nails. Odd that anyone who talks to her for an extended period of time starts scratching their head, too—people around her, colleagues, the cuckoo birds.

Rosa. Reflection in the mirror. My face has gotten thicker. Like a person who goes to work. High time to return to life.

I feel how work—any kind of disciplined work with rules and colleagues—exhausts me. It sucks out the marrow and the innards. Picks them out to make soup.

The Great One remembers how when he started school as a child, he was excited to meet friends, but at the same time felt he wasn't *himself* around other kids.
Rosa feels it when she's alone with Son for a long time and then has to go back to work. Among the cuckoos.

Rosa. We have fun together, eating, drinking, talking trash, yelling—but then when I'm alone again, I realize it was utter chaos. Of another world. A flaming comet with long wild hair. Apparently tied in a ponytail. And I'm surprised that our silliness, that debauchery and revelry, which I admittedly initiated myself, didn't cause any accidents. Or tragedy.

The *odd school of life*[2]. Merriment as neurosis. Humor as war.

And, all the while, as if I were a swimmer, it's clear to me that there's nothing more dangerous than having a laughing fit when you're in the water. You have trouble keeping your head above water. Waves wash over your face.

Today I read that they found the dead body of a Japanese tourist in the Danube. He jumped from Novy Most into the river. His Japanese friends said he jumped *for fun*.

Who knows how many twists and turns of the river it lasted…a Japanese animé joke.

---

2   All italicized text in this book are quotations or are spoken or sung by someone else.

My grandmother, before going to sleep, before turning off the light, terrified, but with joy: *So we'll survive, won't we? Then we'll survive after all...*

When she was in a good mood, Rosa's first boss called her employees little cuckoos. "How are you today, my little cuckoos?"

Rosa. Cuckoos, what a phenomenon—women who fill every day of my world. Uninvited guests. The bottomless stamina of cuckooness. They've always got something to say, to shout, to prattle about.

(Work, children, family, money, music, family, children, work, food, cognac, sex, plastic surgery, political theories, cellulite on the walls, food, cognac, work, money, sex, cellulite.)

At wit's end, writes Camus.

I escape from work. On the dark street, I run into Son. After a long drought, we suddenly kiss on the sidewalk.

Tequila is so powerful, it outshines life.

Like the stars—
It throws into the air
All the crumbs.

We have coffee. The wintery city grips us like a steel trap. Hüzün. We get on the train to Vienna. Just to be inside something that's MOVING.

It moves farther and farther away. Weg! Weg!

So we'll survive, won't we? We'll survive after all...

Rosa's first boss, the little captain, always acted distracted. It was supposed to draw attention away from her purposeful deeds. She was always losing her knife, so she could pat her pockets and mumble, got my knife, got my knife. Got my wallet, got my mobile, got my keys, got my knife.

The little captain was the archetype of a cuckoo. She devoured the space with her overflowing energy, all around her a kind of shivering gelatin spread, muddying the air. She made things opaque.

She was forever clutching a small animal under her arm. She always dressed him differently, so sometimes it was a dog, other times a wolf, a raven, a mouse, a reindeer, a dolphin or a pangasius.

It was her sweetie. It threw up under other people's desks and peed on their backpacks, purses, feet. The little captain placed it on the table during meals and it ate from plates and nibbled at crumbs. Everyone thought it was funny, it was *so cute, such a sweetie*. And the little captain would shout: Is it bothering you? Oh, I'm so glad it's OK with you!

The animal was extremely loved.

Just as ogres' hearts are found in the golden eggs laid by geese, the little captain's heart was in her pet. The other cuckoos nicknamed her clown beast.

The clown beast's smile and roaring laughter wafting through the forest: that was what held Rosa prisoner. She didn't want to run away from a laughing person. From a cackling cuckoo.

In reality, the laughter made her legs turn to wood. Her calves and wrists quivered. In reality, Rosa was immobilized. She couldn't even lie down, she was so completely frozen.

Everything became more dramatic on the day before Christmas. The little captain walked into the room. Under her arm, the animal was dressed as a boy. Just like Son.

Rosa took it into her arms, squeezed it and threw it out the window.

Standing in the doorway, she patted her pockets and mumbled:
Got my feet—got my hands.
Got my knife.

We can go.

In January, taking a walk is useless. You start to feel—enveloped in the gray and grief of lifeless nature—as if you were in a grave. Among the frozen, naked trees, under a nonexistent sky, surrounded by icy earth mimicking the dirty footprints of people—a grave. Except the corpse is missing. There's just a rock, a rock under the ground.

All that's left is how to choose the most aesthetic suicide: marriage + 9 to 5 office job, or a revolver. Camus develops this further.

Rosa gets scared that she won't be able to keep walking. Her useless steps freeze. A tiny heart attack. In the middle of the road. She pulls out her telephone and calls her brother. Her legs hear a new, but familiar voice. The voice of a child. The eternal conversation of an older brother and younger sister. The legs continue thoughtlessly on. Swinging on the sides of trotting reindeer.

Rosa. The bridge. Weariness. If somebody pushed me, I'd fall over like a heavy sack. Right onto the sidewalk. The sack would come undone. Its contents tumbling into the water.

The tunnel. Dripping with icicles. They reach from above toward the hot crown of the head.

Oh, let me, let me, let me freeze again.

"Prose talks about something; poetry makes it happen with the help of words."
People are divided into two groups, poets and prose writers. Into Sons and Rosas.

That's why the first question strangers ask at the breakfast table is: And do you write poetry or prose? Anywhere in the world. At any literary festival.

And then there's a sea of nodding heads and pops of small tubs of butter, jam and honey opening.

And the conclusion is always that prose is fine, but the best, of course, is poetry.

Prose writers will fight for this with their entire morphological lexicon.

And then they will take their last bites and go up to their rooms.

Have you ever looked under the cushion of a chair in a hotel room where novelists and poets stayed? You'd find a bleating herd of crumbs.

Blindness. Black dots everywhere. Birds flying past the window. The window of the bus.

Son. I thought they were gunk on the window or a flock of birds. Crows. Ravens? How long does it take to accept: they're inside your eye. They're flying inside your eye.

(*Oh, birds…*)

Rosa. The second time it happened, they flew into the apartment building. At night. Just that day, Son had bought a book he'd been dying to read his whole life. Since puberty at least, when he'd discovered Albert Camus. *The Notebooks—Carnets*. He read it in an armchair in a house full of sleeping people. Black flocks began to attack the text. More and more birds, fewer words. Blindness had grown wings.

Rosa again. Slovakia. This country, these people—no inspiration.

My friend Gergana was telling me: you should go out more, meet some people…

Go out and meet people? What PEOPLE?

Gergana is not a Slovak and her name always reminds me of Gorgon. Medusa.

You hear yourself, how you're pronouncing phrases and words that don't go together. You don't create them, you just repeat what was said somewhere else, sometime, definitely hanging in the air. Empty, translucent bubbles.

Like Odysseus. *No-body*.

Like when the sea blooms.

(A sign that somewhere in the vicinity there must be a cuckoo.)

And there's only one way to save yourself.

Pat your pockets in the doorway and mumble:
Feet, hands, knife.

After several eye operations, Son sits in the hospital courtyard in his patient's pajamas. Today he's going home. He can hardly see anything at all.

No-body starts to cry.

Son. Don't worry, I won't burden you.

Echo. A burden...a burden. A burden

The retinas are healing. The birds are nowhere to be seen.

Risk. A trip to Berlin. Son says: the only things I've been able to recognize in this room are the big pumpkins with glowing eyes—Halloween.

They were still lighting up the room from All Saints Day.

Son is in a café in Berlin—"*jednu kááávu prosíím*". He pronounces everything slowly and clearly like a polite foreigner to a person who's trying to learn his language. As if he thought everyone should understand Slovak if a person speaks clearly, loudly and emphatically.

After our return, we sit in a Czech pub eating goulash and drinking beer. Lent is coming to an end—it's the Thursday before Easter. The film is ripping, the black dots in front of his eyes growing bigger. Like hockey pucks on the ice.

They're on my face. I must have chosen my seat badly. The worst place. Directly opposite Son.

We run to the hospital. The doctor and nurses are just leaving for the long Easter weekend. The doctor orders the operating room sterilized again. The anesthesiologist isn't there anymore, the doctor mixes the drug cocktail himself. When no one's looking, his colleague leans over to Son and reproachfully whispers: You picked a hell of a time for an operation!

Jesus caused problems right on Easter, too.

Rosa returns to the apartment for Son's pajamas. She lies face down on the carpet. Howling.

After a few minutes, she rises with renewed strength. This is how it works when you're twenty-five.

Evening, Gergana. Even if he went blind, you'd still love him, wouldn't you?
And take him out?
Take him out to meet PEOPLE.

ON THE ROAD

And, if on the way to the hospital or in the forest I should meet a cuckoo. If I've already seen her from afar, as she prepares to throw herself at me in friendship, love, and conversation. In an embrace. I beat her to it—in that instant when she pauses to gather her bile—I lunge at her and plant a big kiss on each of her cheeks. Then I push her away and resume my journey.

It's such a militant mode of defense. To kiss, embrace and then *shove* someone as far away as possible.

That humiliating feeling, when you stand face to face with a cuckoo and you feel yourself adapting. You smile, kiss. You do the cuckoo thing. There's nothing for it—to face the cuckoos unveiled, that would be to risk exposure to radiation. To risk damage. Explosions, things flying everywhere, saliva, grimaces, teeth.

That's why when I go face to face with a cuckoo, I become a cuckoo, too. I purse my lips, open my eyes wide, offer my cheeks. Cuckoo-cuckoo-cuckoo.

Son in the hospital. After the operation, the positioning phase. For the retina to heal, the patient has to lie for as long as they can face down. Toward the ground.

Away! Away!

He comes home with a black patch over his left eye. Son the pirate. Mister Pirateson.

Something fell into his eye.

(January?)

Camus says that wind is one of the few pure things in the world. Not in the city, not in Lapa. The spring wind is a garbage collector.

It drives the dust, relics of thousand-year-old dirt toward wide open eyes. To lidless, spring eyes.

Kai?

The poet says that a day spent indoors is lost.

A situation. Rosa and Pirateson are talking in the kitchen. In the middle of the discussion, he suddenly gets up and goes into the other room.
Rosa. Don't go away yet! Stay here with me, please.
Son. I'm not going into the other room.
Rosa. No?
Son. I'm going into *myself*. I'd like to live alone now, Rosa. Alone in the apartment. I should leave, but I don't have enough money, Rosa.
Not money nor an eye.

prose & poetry

Rosa, March 2009. January is lasting too long. A bad habit. When she comes home she stays dressed for outdoors. She warms up some food with hat on head, opens a bottle of wine with coat on.

Rosa. I grew up like a seeing-eye dog. That's the kind of training I have.

To this day, I freeze when I hear my master's voice. To this day, when I walk beside someone, I look ahead, into the distance, to protect them against every unevenness in the pavement, every pothole.

I lift and levitate him, in places I navigate him like a pilot.

What could possibly happen next? I say aloud to myself in the empty apartment. Who knows.
Or, as Grandma used to say:
Whonose.

The cuckoos are always exhausted. Faking it is equally draining as actual effort. Going through life forever flustered, endlessly surprised at how things turn out. And then there's the fear that someone will come along and utter the truth: she's a fake. But of course, that's never happened, and most cuckoos remain firmly flustered into their forties.

Of course, in addition to this, there are always more and more cuckoos coming of age somewhere.

During another extreme cold spell, she goes to feed the animals in the zoo. The zebras' feet slip out from under them on the ice, the giraffes don't come out at all. She meets a rhinoceros. The zookeeper says she can touch it without a problem. Apparently, it's one of the few animals that doesn't find being pet by a human unpleasant. She hesitantly places her palm on the gray skin. Like the bark of a sycamore. Healing contact with a warm and peaceful planet.

Gergana wrote a short story about lovers and alcohol. During a life-changing night, the woman turns her back on *it*, but he doesn't. He remains with the bottle.

He. I just think that in the story you demonize alcohol too much. After all, we've had so many beautiful times with *it*…
She. But I hope we would have had those times *without it too*…
He. I don't know, I'm not so sure about that…

Whonose.

Son. That guy should go under the psychiatrist's knife.

Have some more. One more glass before bed.

No thank you, I'll have something else.

What?

A glass of water, recently I've started drinking a glass of water before bed.

A glass of water? Before bed? Now that would really kill me!

The party at Chapter's house was finishing up and everyone was gradually escaping, old Mr. Klaus Chapter was quite drunk. Son signaled to those leaving that they need not worry about Chapter, that he would stay with him. He also saw out three of Klaus's adult children. In the meantime, the old man began urgently looking for something in the library. He lost his balance and hit his head hard on a metal construction. Blood streamed down his face toward the chin.

"Come, I have to clean your wound," Son said, pulling him into the bathroom. Chapter stood over the sink and his eyes met those in the mirror. Under his own smashed up forehead. With blood.

"Son, we were outside too…? No?"
(silence)
And who else is here besides the two of us…? Nobody?
(a longer silence)

So YOU did this to me? YOU beat me up? I never would have thought you could be such a Stalinist!

In his old age, the Great One started building a stone tower by the lake. He lived there without modern conveniences—he brought water from the well, and heated the place with firewood.

He claimed that our consciousness—our souls inherited from our ancestors—can viscerally react to our circumstances. And when they're unhappy with our modern lifestyle, this manifests in our feeling unwell. The Great One built the tower so there would be nothing strange or unknown, even to a person who stumbled in from the 16th century, except maybe for the lamps and matches. Thanks to this, he had various visitors.

When Klaus Chapter died, in the room where he had lived for 30 years—the last 10 sick and the very last one dying—his children placed a computer. Exactly where his bed had been.

The computing center replaced death.

Rosa. When I was running away, I used a small computer from Austria. It was like a crippled old man. Slow, not connected to the Internet. Moreover, I couldn't change the keyboard from the German one to one with accents, and so I wrote without them. *All wrong.*

Crippled machines have great charm. For example, Walkmans were invaluable during socialism. We used them until they fell apart, their cassette doors secured with the thick rubber band one could find on a canning jar. The jack on the earphones always broke so that only one earphone worked. To make it stereo again, we had to seal it in place. Like a piece of ham in aspic.

Over time, every Walkman in the socialist bloc became a vintage original. The design emerged from the repairs done by the owner, his family & friends.

Rosa. Some praise cities—Paris, London, Prague. For me, however, nature is more important—oceans, mountains—God's country. Separation from it results in anguish and grief. Especially in January. In the city, there are no images that console me.

Son chooses some old pants from the closet.

Rosa. They have holes in them.

Son. No matter, it's windy.

Son and Rosa on a trip to Budapest. In the bookshop window: Marx Karoly, Verne Gyula, Shakespeare Vilmos.

The sculptor in a pub. He sits alone at a table for six, it's Friday, three o' clock in the afternoon, on his third cognac. From time to time, he pulls out his mobile with the touch screen, sometimes he twists the ring on his little finger and then gradually tries to put it on all the other fingers…hands…

Lapa. Naked in the bathtub. Morning. Conversation in the hallway.

I'm giving you one last chance to act like a human being.
Shut up, you fucking faggot, or I'll pound you right here!
So hit me, you old prick, and I'll fuck you up so bad…!
AGGHHHHH….who's gonna help you here? Who's gonna help you?

Lapa. That's the worst thing about it: the only one who can hear you is a naked woman in the bathtub.

Who's gonna help you, you asshole, huh? Nobody. No one gives a fuck. We can do whatever we want. Because here, nobody, nobody will help anybody.

And I look for him in vain: *No-body* isn't anywhere. *No-body* is gooooone.

MAGNUM

"And Mrs. Kaminsky is bringing water from the river!" cries the cuckoo. She is organizing a book signing for a book about a famous actor, Max Kaminsky. He's 100 years old. From far away, he's still attractive. As times goes on, from farther and even farther away. They'll baptize the book with water from the river.

Kaminsky is trying to say something, but the audience can't hear anything. There's either an issue with him or with the microphone. His young wife is sitting in the third row shouting at him: Max, microphone! Closer to your mouth. Like a Magnum ice cream bar! Like a Magnum, Max!

Rosa escaped from Son and Lapa on September 11th before 5:00 in the morning. He was sleeping. She left a note: I've fallen in love with another man. The wedding we were planning is off. We've already been bride and groom. And had a wedding. A long time ago. Sometime. A hundred years ago.

A hundred years ago. She had gotten sick and Son secretly stole into her parents' house. She was in the house taking care of her grandmother with Alzheimer's. Her parents were still working. The neighbors, however, monitored all activity on their street. Neighbors. Dogs. Every foreigner was noted. Son slipped in. With chocolate of gargantuan proportions. Instead of armor. Although her doctor had said no sex for a couple of days, they made love sitting on the couch. For a moment, on the other side of the doors with so-called frosted glass windows, she caught her grandmother's silhouette. Grandma was pacing back and forth in the hall.

Rosa. When Son left, she asked me who that man was, because she thought she knew what we were doing. When I asked what, she answered: *meditating.* She had never used that word before.

That was the wedding. Bride, groom, and grandmother behind frosted glass.

And wedding music, sung by a freshly deceased singer from a tape. He'd died a few days before I met Son:

my absence touches me
your absence touches me
her fingers...

Rosa. If only someone had written such words for me that I could use to so vividly complain after death.

A few days later, Son's sister got married. He traveled to the wedding and when Rosa came home, he was still sleeping off a night of partying. She touched him under the covers and he reacted like a newlywed. When they got up, they shared a piece of cake. A wedding favor. With the remains of the figurines on top.

Rosa. Then I pulled three pins out of my mouth one at a time.

I guess they were holding the figurines in place, said Son.

A hundred years later, Rosa rises from their common bed and runs for the train to Vienna and beyond. Eventually to Krems. From Son to Corman. She considers Krems her birthplace. She once had her own apartment there, for the first and last time.

Rosa. In those days, when I missed Son, I would find myself at the train station.

And then he came.

Despite everything. She felt that Krems held even more potential. The potential of a new man. Who was already waiting. He was growing up somewhere, just for her. From something, some tangible material, from her own rib. From her vagina, membranes, lips, tongue, saliva and slivers of soil from the vineyards.

Rosa. He's growing from the most hidden and softest parts of my own self. Wild flesh. My own desire.

Behind frosted glass.

To get to Krems, she takes the regional express from Vienna. But first she has to get to another train station. The subway journey takes her under nearly the entire city. Arriving at the other station, she sees no train to Krems announced on the departures board. She asks a station employee how to get to Krems. The woman slowly swallows a mouthful of croissant. "They're repairing the railroad bridge. You have to take the train to Tulln, transfer there to a bus, and then catch the train to Krems." Rosa thanks her. A text message beeps on her phone. From Son. Telling her that he read her note and that he had suspected as much, and good luck. Her body contorts as she weeps. She covers her face at least. With both hands. And moves away from the woman toward the end of the platform. When she uncovers her eyes, she sees that the woman is looking at her with surprise. Thinking Rosa hasn't understood her. That she probably has trouble with German. That she's worried she's gotten lost. She's wandered. Wandered off her path.

She weeps on the railway platform. And realizes that it's a good place. One can cry on platforms and in stations, after all, since people come here to say goodbye. To see off their loved ones. To be left alone. To kiss each other and rip their lips apart. To wait in vain. Or get off a train quite unnecessarily.

Rosa. I'm thinking of Corman's small, boy's mouth. Firmly pressed on mine. The lower lip doesn't want to separate from mine, even in sleep.

How often novelists write about it, when they want to describe intense passion: they began to kiss hungrily. We kissed each other with precision. Solemnly.

When I think of it, I still can't catch my breath.

The railroad workers gather those traveling to Krems at Tulln and put them on a bus. They look worriedly at my face, swollen from weeping. Like the reindeer at Gerda.

On the bus, I get the best seat. Right behind the driver.

A person grows fragile on the road, on trains, buses and again on trains. Like a tin soldier.

He eats little. Doesn't sleep enough. The setting: high alert. He awaits orders. Images. Unexpected incidents. Sometimes he dreams: the pub, his bed, his lover, an illness.

The railroad ties rhythmically hit his feet. The floor of the train shakes.

Trains and love. An excellent combination.

At the station. A girl leans against the radiator. She's making a call from a phone booth. She hangs up. Weeping. Leans her forehead against the telephone.

As Son is doing at home.

We weren't born for this: We can't just fall down somewhere, anywhere on the side of the road. And cry a river.

Collapse? For that you need a psychiatrist.

He still believes in signs. Like August Strindberg. When Strindberg traveled to see his own plays, he was always very nervous. Until the moment when, standing in the aisle of the train by the window, he saw the sign on the incoming train flash by: Victoria August.

Rosa. Just before Son and I left Paris last summer, I noticed a discarded plastic glove on the road. When we passed it, the wind filled the fingers, making a 'V' for Victory.

DOGWALKERS

My American uncle was a key figure for me. Visits to his house are forever linked in my mind to big life challenges. Son and I went to Paris because he needed someone to dog-sit. In our family, dogs were always associated with unruliness and unpredictability. With betrayal and treachery. All the dogs that ever appeared in our yard were beasts. They went for the jugular. On the other hand, they were always the most beautiful dogs in the whole neighborhood. When we went on vacation, our Cocker Spaniel Caruso chased the neighbor who came to feed him twice a day into the pantry. She lived in there until the day we returned. The dog had shiny golden fur, after a week in the pantry the neighbor went gray.

It's a good dog, a bit fat and spoiled by medicines. After the uncle moved from America to Paris, and brought the dog with him, animal depression set in. He had been a happy American boy, but in the Paris apartment, he lay under the sink like a black rag.

The rag was interested only in eating and masturbating. In those moments, the playfulness and vitality of the *American in Paris* would return.

"Slow on the leash, pallid the leash-men!"

Visits with the uncle were always full of opportunity—yet required embodying *No-body*. When Rosa was fifteen, she flew to visit him in America. It was her first trip to the West—and her first trip ever.

She flew to America from Prague, changed planes in Frankfurt and London. The flight had a big delay and the trip took longer than 24 hours. When she got off the plane in Los Angeles, for a moment she had no idea why she had actually come or whether someone was supposed to be waiting for her. (*No-body?*) Is this what it looks like out in the world?

Away! Away!

On the airplane, she met a traveler who was like a character out of the Odyssey. A young woman from Prague who spent every summer holiday with her uncle in America, making her the envy of everyone. During socialism, uncles in America were mythical characters.

In reality, however, she spent the summer in a small town hanging around her uncle's garage. He was an auto mechanic. She never learned any English because her uncle and his family were happy they could speak Czech with her.

Rosa took *Crime and Punishment* with her to the American mountains. While reading it, she babysat for her three-year-old nephew.

The uncle in America always lived in a kingdom—San Francisco, Petrograd, Milan, New York, Paris. There was always something untameable and wild in it. A big spider, a small boy, a dog. And Rosa was supposed to take care of it. In each kingdom, they spoke a different language. She tried to deal with it. Someone once said that you can converse in a foreign language, but you can never speak it. In a foreign language, a person is cursed, like *No-body*. They can't be themselves—they don't expand—they just sink inward.

IN PARIS

After a month in Paris, Son has trouble remembering some Slovak word. That's so us—we've forgotten our own language and haven't learned the foreign one.

No-body. For years we've only talked amongst ourselves. Linguistic incest.

In Paris. I spear the green lettuce with a big sharp knife and put it in my mouth. Exactly like my father does at home with bacon.

The same noble style.

In Paris, something devours the time. Maybe it's the metro cars. Maybe it's the constant walking around the city. Or that dog that's always hungry. He growls at cucumbers and the poop of his canine compatriots. He likes to eat paper tissues and cake, which I went all the way to the Jewish quarter to buy and then left out within his reach. Boom! That's what happens to a soldier when he's not on his guard.
In Paris. It's useless to fixate on pastries.

In Paris, every minute has only a few seconds, something here swallows up the time. Digests it. I guess that's why people here love extremely fresh baguettes. They prefer to put them under their arm—directly from the oven—with a hint of flame still burning. In Paris.

In Paris, I have two kinds of salt on the table. One with bigger and one with smaller crystals. Luxury.

In Paris, chestnuts don't lose their shine.

They glow like the dark brown heart on my necklace. It reminds the cuckoos of a chocolate gingerbread cookie. It reminds me of gym equipment—leather, mats, horse. Something I never managed to jump over.

My friend, who's lived here for years and speaks Slovak with an accent, has two sons. She says that their apartment is a little small for two children. *"But the boys are very well-loved."*

In Paris. The windows are as big as the door.

In the dimness of the metro the nightlife is non-stop.

In Paris. In the morning, half asleep, Son traces a circle with his fingers on his chest. For lunch, there's meat in a spicy sauce. He sweats over the plate like a woman in labor with her first-born. *Very well-loved.*

In Bratislava, on the day we came back from Paris. We're sitting on a bench in the park. Lost. Helpless. Feeling sorry for ourselves. As if someone close to us had died.

Paris in Paris.

During a bombardment in Budapest, the novelist sits in his apartment and wonders what he would regret never experiencing—seeing the ocean, walking in Paris...

For me, Krems.

Corman at the station. A little shorter than me. I fasten myself to his lips. I get a bouquet of flowers. Freshly wrapped in paper. Like popcorn.

A hundred years ago. Son and I began to date in the fall. A brutal winter followed. Spicy. Snow and ice. For months, the path he accompanied me down every night to my parents' house was covered in a thick, lumpy layer of ice.

"I wasn't born for this, to walk on ice," I burst into tears once in the middle of the street.

In Krems there's a room available at the *Golden Angel* hotel.

A morning message from Son. Sorry, but I'm afraid I'm dying. He'd never used that word before. Something like my grandmother and the word *meditation*.

I call him, with Corman's ear on my hip. In my belly, a small animal sobs. A big gathering storm.

Behind the frosted glass, there's thunder and lightning. Like backstage at the marionette theater.

ROME, ROTHKO

Rome, sometime. An exhibit of Rothko's paintings. And Son, who is dragging me from one picture to another. And intermittently covering one eye with his hand. With his left he sees only light and dark. ("I can brighten it up.") And suddenly the monochrome colors lighten up or dim down. He stands in front of the painting, his hand clutching my elbow, and shouts at me: Look! Look! It's so odd how I see it now! And he looks at the pictures with only the brightening eye.

"But, Son, I can't look at it that way. I don't have one half-blind eye."
"Agh," he laughs, "that's too bad! What a shame!"
And a few paintings later he adds: "Sorry. Sorry, Rosa."

We walk through the streets of Rome. It's raining. I ask him several times not to hold onto my elbow as we're walking. And he looks at me with shocked eyes. Brightening me up. Until I burst into tears.

Lovers never lead each other around by the elbow. Only blind people. And puppets. And to the executioner.

(I wasn't born for this, to be led around by the elbow.)

Rothko said somewhere that he had a problem showing some of his paintings. It seemed risky to him to exhibit them in front of insensitive eyes. He knew that such looks could seriously damage the canvas. He'd rather *No-body* saw them.

KREMS, NOW

She decides to run back. To comfort Son. To interrupt her journey. She's drinking wine with Corman, it's almost lunchtime. A bit drunk, they walk up—to the highest point in town—to the vineyards. This is Rosa's road. Through the woods. She always found this healing. So far, she's shared it with only two men. Both of them lagged, breathing hard.

They weren't born for this, to walk up hills.

Corman has sweated out his Riesling. He smells like a little dog. Fruity.

Near the wood they pass a house that reminds them of a gingerbread hut. Inside, in the semi-darkness, sits an old woman. Corman calls to her, greets her, smiles, and approaches the fence. The old woman lights up and on her swollen, bright red legs comes to meet him. As if to some old lover she'd been awaiting for years. Like the uncle in America. They smile at each other. Corman tells her that she has a beautiful house.

She gestures to him that she can't come any closer. Her legs are leaden.

Rosa. "Das ist mein Haus," Someone calls from behind us.

We greet a married couple, Grüsgot.
Grüsgot.

Grüsgot.

Grüsgots. They look at us a bit severely. I guess our eyes didn't seem sensitive enough. Not sensitive enough to inspect their house.

Farther up there's a bench. Three years ago, I would come here to read Son's *Little Book*.

Now, I caress Corman under his t-shirt.

A few steps beyond the bench I dig a shallow hole. I put my mobile phone in it and cover it with dirt.

And then, further. The road. From Krems to Melk. After a couple of glasses of red wine, around midnight. Night and a fast, steady ride. (A gallop?) Our palms are crossed on each other's thighs. The ends of our fingers are dusted with gold. In another universe. A twin planet is hurtling along.

We're a two-headed dragon, Son whispers somewhere in the distance. And we still haven't met a knight clever enough to take off one of our heads.

Though some have tried…

GABRIEL

In Melk, we stay at the *Goldener Schlüssel*.

Again. After years I find my mouth. On Corman's collar bone. Below his waist.

Nothing can replace a kiss. The mouth is a small body, a large brain. (Taste, breath, connection. Everything. Essential.)

Taking a walk in the morning. I walk past a woman with a dog. After a moment, the dog joins me.

"Gabriel! Gabriel! Heel! Gabriel! That's not me!"

I don't know how we found our way into that courtyard. But there was a museum of harmonicas and accordions there. The owner—Pierre—was also the owner of the puppet theater. That night they were performing *The Snow Queen*.

TWO DAYS LATER, BRATISLAVA

I walk over to Son's. The return. Over the bridge and along the terrace—through a wasteland. Through the Steppe. The loose cobblestones play under my feet. Geysers of old, dark water spray up into my face. As if from a well. A poisoned one.

We're a two-headed dragon. And we still haven't met a knight clever enough to take off one of our heads.

Unless one turns against the other.

Corman's shining face is moving toward me. Blue eyes with gold flecks in them. Glittering. I count how many knives are waiting for me in my former household. And in what places.

To the north, just keep going. Always moving north, north…

The dogs are growling. Baring their teeth. Love.

Pierre's *Snow Queen* wasn't the best. The reindeer was too decrepit, ethereal. And I had always remembered him as the protector. A Sherpa with a warm voice. And Gerda yelled too much: Kaiiiiii! Kaiiiiiii! Kaiiiiiiii! Just like some schoolteacher.

She yelled louder and louder. But, no, it's the other way around. At that moment, the voice gets more and more muffled, it disappears into the soft snow. Into the drifts on your palate. Why all that yelling?

No-body anywhere.

A familiar head disappeared under a hood.

Gerda was a timid volcano. Little ones, do you have any idea what that could be?

Lapa. I ride the elevator with some young hyped-up neighbor girls. I have the feeling that a glass wall has risen around me. A sack. Frosted glass. Nothing can affect me. Lapa has lost its power. It can't touch me anymore. It won't get to me. Burrow inside. After all these years here, these girls have been sucked out of my world in a second. We ride together through the dark building, I look indifferently and directly at their unattractive, pudgy teenage faces. Lapian faces. They seem so eternal. As if they'd stepped out of a Terry Gilliam film. And he's a big expert on monsters.

Summer in Bratislava. Son never wants to sit outside at the café tables. "I can't just sit down here on the street in summer and pretend to be relaxed. As if I were suddenly on vacation in some resort. I can't." On these empty, inhospitable streets, where we wander all year round. We stagger around, soul-less.

Don't go anywhere! Stay here! Where are you going!
Just go then! Just go!
Grrrgrrrgrrrr.

IMMER DA

Morning in Melk. Church bells. Too loud. Catholic heavy metal. Corman, sitting in the open window, smoking and chortling. On the wall opposite there's a billboard, an ad for God. "Whenever the ground gets shaky under your feet. Don't forget! Ich bin immer da für dich, Gott.[3]

You slowly open your eyes, in a long kiss. Pupils wide like after an intense drug cocktail.

---

3   Translation: I'm always there for you, God.

Trains like reindeer. Galloping through the countryside.

Animals without bells, bells without animals.

Son is talking. I remember that I could relate to all the characters in that fairytale. Except for the Snow Queen. I didn't like Kai. A puppet. A little boy-princess. But I could have been the reindeer, the raven, Gerda or the Little Captain. Or Kai in Gerda and Gerda in Kai.

Rosa. I bought myself two white t-shirts. Instead of a wedding dress.

Lapa, the apartment, inside. In Son's room. Corman's eyes glow like lanterns. Son is saying that he doesn't want to know anything. No details. Only whether the guy is Slovak.
I tell him he's an extraterrestrial.

E.T.

Well then I'm fucked, says Son.

THE INFINITY SIGN

The road continues to Graz and Klagenfurt. Bicycles in the city, some of them with crazily bent wheels—firmly locked on the side of the street. So that no one steals them. And takes off down that crooked road. A fantastical route littered with infinity signs.

Corman stands in the window naked and lithe. Smoking.

While they sleep, he holds Rosa by the feet. Like a bicycle by the pedals.

Hotel *Goldene Pastete.*[4]

On the medicine cabinet in the bathroom is the word GOD. Except instead of an 'O', they've used a droplet.

Austria is that kind of country. Everything is GOLDENE.

And it's all about GOD.

And the geraniums thrive. Waterfalls of them. They choke all the windows. Like cancer. Blooming.

---

4   Translation: Hotel Golden Paté.

A country of Grüsgots.

Pierre says that Gerda is chasing the evil in Kai. That's why the journey is so sad. Rosa thinks that the frost is the worst thing about it anyway. After all, when the Little Captain imprisons Gerda in her friendship and then lets her go, she only leaves Gerda her hat. Her scarf and gloves she keeps, she can't resist.

To the north. Always moving north…

I live inside myself like in a moving train.

Rosa says: I wasn't born for this—to play Gerda.

Corman is quite a short man, a few centimeters shorter than me. And Pierre is half a head shorter than him again. Whenever I look at him, instinctively—somewhere in the back of my head and the pit of my stomach—I wonder if he's just a small man or actually a dwarf. Where is the line?

And you, what do you write? Prose or poetry?

(Jam or marmalade?)

We drink wine from Kras and eat cured ham all night. It tastes like sea air. We smoke. Pierre wants to join us on the road. He admires Corman's massive car. Though his is more luxurious, shinier and faster—he can't fit all his puppets and sets into it. He's been dreaming for years about going on tour.

With *The Snow Queen.*

Drunk, they begin to pack the puppet theater into Corman's car during the night. They fill the seats with wooden figures. The windows are boarded up from the inside with scenery. The car as ark. As coffin. With the owner of the puppet theater—the biggest doll of all—on the deck.

A puppet. Deadly.

Now you look quite like the Little Prince. You know that character, don't you? Corman turns to me. Our car is filled to the brim. There's nowhere for me to sit anymore.

There's just a small air bubble for the driver. Like a knot in the wood.

IN TOW

They seat me in Pierre's car. We will ride the whole way in tow. Us in front and Corman behind us.

On the road.

Sometimes Son's back flashes before our eyes. Always as a pedestrian, eternally car-less. As if Pierre were kidnapping me or taking me back.

Slovenia is up ahead.

The car moves faster and faster. Like a golden coach. Golden horses glitter before us and everything around us is suddenly GOLDENE.

Pierre is an old man. But behind the wheel, he suddenly feels that his body, like the functioning machine, should rev up as well. Sophisticatedly. Smoothly. The way it's supposed to. Onward! (North. Always north.) Like a reindeer.

Or a raven.

No-body?

At a certain moment, he offers the wheel to me. I make excuses, saying that I'm used to driving a different kind of car, a small, imperfect, disobedient one.

Pierre. Once you become a driver, you can drive any car. It's like with women. They all have stuff in the same place.
Actually, it's the opposite, Pierre. Actually.

He tries to touch me.

I tell him I wasn't born for that.

He tells stories, never taking his eyes off the windshield and the landscape beyond, and they all end in fucking, humping, or at least sex.

In many of them, wives escape at dawn from their husbands, destroying them. For life.

Pierre is precisely that kind of character. *The kind that doesn't exist, but leads us into insanity, gets us in a chokehold.*

Slovenia. Sun, cloudless sky, the road, mountains, crystal clear air, a glittering feeling. Freedom!

I look in the rear-view mirror. Under the car seat my legs are stubbornly turning to wood.

Lonely, so lonely is the dreaming child.

AWAY!

Never let them take your leg!
Arthur Rimbaud

CHOOOOOBOOOOOOOOH

Last winter, Rosa and Son watched Kurosawa films. Every night, one after the other. They drank wine and watched: the little boy Chobo steals something and his parents are so ashamed that they decide to bring their poverty to an end once and for all, to fix the situation. They poison themselves and their children with a meal made from poisonous mushrooms.

Chobo is in the hospital dying and the Japanese women, to sustain his soul and distract death run out to the well in the courtyard and call down into the dark hole in the Earth: Chooobooooh, Choooooboooooh!

Rosa. That winter, Son and I called each other Chobo, Chobinko, Choooo-booooh.

I told Pierre who the puppet masters are in my country. The people who couldn't get into a real theater. They have too little talent and drink too much alcohol. Or they've lived through some life trauma that threw them off course. Into a ditch. A ditch full of tears and puppets. Furry and tangled with strings and fibers.

Away! Away!

Pierre. In our country, it's a person who can do a little of every-thing—sing, dance, act, write, paint. A little. A lick.

We will stop in the town of Velenje. Supposedly there is an interesting painting there.

Two cats on a highway. Nighttime. One is lying on the shoulder. Hit by a car. The second is sitting by it, mouth open toward the heavens in silent pain. Full of pointy teeth. Instead of stars. Like ammunition. An empty road. Behind them. In front of them. Only the omnipresent dotted white line.

Ich bin immer da...für dich.

A text from Son. Chooobooh! Only that darkness awaits me now. In the well. I must prepare for it.

At home. She started smoking again. Corman's brand with a white filter. The only ones she, as a non-smoker, likes. As light as a scam.

At home. Trains. Painfully absent. Movement, sound. The Alps through the window. Foreigners, who you sit with, thigh to thigh. Sleeping lovers who stretch out too much. In his hand, he holds her foot in a white—marital—sock.

At home. That odd obsession with shoes. It gripped her all last spring. She bought two pairs of Gortex boots—with specially reinforced toes. For extreme conditions.

She's just finished reading Vrba's book *I Escaped from Auschwitz.* She was preparing her own escape. The road.

Vrba claims it's the <u>shoes</u> that are the most important thing when escaping. And only then food and water.

And what about feet?

An old poster from the 1989 revolution on our cupboard reads PERSIST! (Ich bin immer da…?)
Blue lettering on yellowed paper.

Next to the poster, a scene from Pinocchio—an angry owner of a puppet theater with flames reflected in his pupils. Teeth jutting from his lips. With a tuft of hair. He's holding four puppets on strings. They wait for his attack. Cowering. At the same time, they shield their faces against the fire burning just below the stage. A cap from one of them has already caught fire and blown away. Flown off its wooden head.

Son. Those rich western men... I can't compete with them. With their cars and their money.

Especially in the morning, the flames reach for Rosa's thighs.

They're licking. Inside too.

At home.

I live inside myself like in a moving train.

Your muteness means always...(just a bit) satiating with silent lamb.

When she was quiet again. So disgustingly silent. Dead. A creature without a mouth. Without breath. Son took off her shoes. As if something would change. Life itself. She pulled her bare feet back under herself on the bench. And he, helpless, depressed like a dog by her silence, took her sneakers in his hand and ran his fingers over them.

She remembered how, years back, when he had gone away for a few days and in the entranceway had left his—no longer needed at the moment—winter boots. She thrust her hands into them up to the wrists.

Then her nose. Cheeks. Finally, her whole face. Up to the neck.

Shoes. A trustworthy signal. An update on who's inside and who's gone out.

Away! Away!

Son narrowly escaped death. I was almost killed by passion. My own.

No-body.

We look the same.

At home.

Son. We're in the same situation. We're both in love. In our bellies summer is peaking. There's no room for appetite.

You see it the most in the eyes, the smoke rising.

People we know tell us how good we look. I remember Artaud. He was complaining to someone: I feel like crap. And the worst thing is that everyone's telling me how good I look.

It shows most in the eyes. I can't stand looking through mine into anyone else's.

Only into the black screen of a mobile phone and the email inbox. Empty nets. Torn. Twisted like my intestines. Into black holes. Both my legs are tied up in them.

Like when we were biking in the summer and suddenly, in front of us, in the middle of the field of cows, there was a fresh asphalt road. We barely braked in time. Half a bike wheel in front of that boiling hot porridge.

Trains and reindeer. I miss those most.

And a hand firmly holding my wrist next to my face. Like a leash.

To the north, always north.

Slow on the leash, pallid the leash-men!

It's a long journey… But in the train. In the train, I'll rest…I take off my shoes. Stretch my legs. A walker in the train. While the countryside runs.

At home. Outside it's raining lightly, autumn. Frightened, Son looks out the window at the fall-colored woods, as if at a blizzard. Like at a tornado. He's telling me how terribly sorry he is that I'll have to go outside. Into that weather. Into any weather. Into the world. Out. Into the abyss. To live. Life.

Our whole apartment. Our burrow that we sit in all day and night in the warmth and look out the window, terrified. Like from the womb. Like from the grave. As if the biggest luck were not to be born at all…

We weren't born for this, to be born…

WITH PIERRE (ON THE ROAD)

We're driving through Lipica. A village that looks like it was bombed. Dead. The only things left are white horses, flies and kilometers of fences. I stagger through them like in a labyrinth. You never know which one will be closed off after a certain time, with a lock and chain. It's quiet. The only sound—a horse's tail hitting a horse's back.

We spend the night in Hotel Cloud. The façade is one big glass wall. I just miss the doorway and run face-first into the glass.

Frosted glass.

In an instant, I feel the heat of my own blood. Streaming, pouring out, spraying. Bubbling like life.

From where?

To where?

The front desk clerk comes running. The blood from my face drips into her décolleté. AGH! she shouts, as if it had burned her.
Bright red.

Finally! Finally! Blood.

And otherwise? *No-body* nowhere.

We crossed through the golden countryside. Into the silver one. Eternal winter. To the bone.

You've just missed your last golden goose.

When a lover disappears, many words emerge that one would still like to say. They stumble around. Falling to the bottom like stones covered with mud. Radioactive waste.

Sometimes a person has to see their own blood. Under their feet on the steps. On the glass wall. On someone else's white skin. Overflowed.

As he sees me off, Pierre wraps me in his hoody. To keep me warm on the train. It's white but dirty. From soil.

I return to Krems. No trace of Corman.

I grow pale. Night after night. The display on my telephone eternally moon-faced.

To the north, always north… I'm brightening up the road. *With my one, blind eye…*

Being personally present is sometimes necessary, essential. Like someone once said at a funeral. Just into a dog's ear.

In the winter, Krems is a ghost town. After dark, there's almost no one there. No one on the streets or in the houses—which resemble set dressing—or in the theater. Only the pavement is real. Made of stones from the Danube. Silence. Silence and, suddenly, accelerated breathing. Running. What's chasing me in this dead town? In my dead hometown. A shadow on the stones and then a young man. *Kai?*

He stops in front of the glass wall of the darkened bank. *No-body?*

He almost runs face first into the wall, but it's opening up in front of him. There is an ATM inside. 24 hours.

That's how night looks in Krems. Corman and I used to laugh at the Greek food stand near the station. It was called *Night Life* and they closed at 7:00pm.

Is it possible that Corman has left me? Is it possible he would leave a woman who introduced him to the night life in Krems?

Did he have a car accident? Did he fall off a cliff? Into the deep water? Slowly he is carried away by it like a puppet in the fire, sparks flying from underneath his wooden cap... Kai? Kaaaaai! No one.

Son claims. He's screaming down the highway and can't find the right exit... He keeps passing the same cars, with the same drivers... All those western men, he can't compete with their cars, their money... He froze... in the burning cold Siberian wave that reached Europe this year.

Son lights a cigarette with a white filter. The marital kind. Son. Interesting, a strange man taught me to smoke again.

Corman's cigarettes. More smoke has been added to our lives.

In the bar. A woman is telling another woman how she practices tantra. Such that the erotic energy flows up through the spine. Her friend disagrees—it's not supposed to do that. It flows up through the heart. Oh, how easy it is to talk about, oh, how easily it flows up through women who aren't fucking anyone at the moment.

It's nice how women know how to support each other in their unhappy romantic entanglements. How they share their sad stories—how men left, disappeared—from their lives. And together they try to figure out what happened—eternally hopeful that they're still loved. It must have been something—something unrelated to love—something that couldn't be helped.

He didn't call? Isn't he a bit spazzy? Or maybe something happened... that's how life goes. For example, the death of a mother...

They probe their collective experiences—memories—like picking through hair for lice.

With tenderness, they look through the locks. Sticking up after a long sleep. Flattened after a long bout of insomnia.

Three weeks ago, she was with Corman in Graz. One night in, suddenly alone, she climbed the steps to the castle and found a bench under a chestnut tree. She lay down on her back and gradually, as the sun brightened, took her clothes off. A sun bath.

I can't make up the fire
The way that she could
I spend all my days
In the search for dry wood.

And suddenly at home. Again.

And then all at once—from day to day—losing the nights—losing meaning, purpose, substance. Especially now in autumn, when, from second to second, they become hours longer. Emptier and emptier. Eeeeeeemptier. Chooooooboooooooh. Chooooobinkooooooh.

Deeper and deeper. More and more hollow. All the way to the core. Of the body. Of the Earth.

I blow into the hollowness, smoke from cigarettes. I pour wine in. Fill it with words. Like a divining rod. Memories of a body. Once already risen. From the dead. From my own saliva; body parts turned inside out, from the soil in the vineyards.

I live inside myself like in a moving train.

A train, from which someone jumped
while it was moving.

MY ROAD TO PORNOGRAPHY AND BACK

All those evenings when I drink nearly an entire bottle of red and dance a lot. My reflection in the dark mirror is my dance partner.

Son watches. Occasionally applauds, offers a thumbs-up…

And the weekends, when one is helpless again, like during puberty. Lying in bed. Alone. As lonely as before one experienced being loved.

Before lovemaking filled all the spaces, pauses, rainy days, all the still moments.

A gallop… reindeer would have something to say about it.

Cleaning, cooking, laundry, weeping.

Gergana. When did it happen? How did it play out? First, he treats you like a goddess, and then suddenly you're like the math teacher he mouths off to?

Whonose.

And those winter afternoons, when, after a couple of lunchtime cognacs, she and Son set out on the road.

Most often it was to New York. They would sit and talk about how they had nothing to lose, they had nothing anyway, so they'd step on the gas. They'd escape from this dead country.

Gergana on her extended family: Whenever we meet, we always drink and buy sailboats. Someone starts about how it's not even that expensive and then there's no stopping it. We dream about pooling our funds and buying a boat. A cruiser or a sailboat.

Only three hundred thousand? We can come up with that, we all shout in turn.

The next morning, we're wandering around the house. No one's talking about sailboats anymore—let alone about water…

Over lunch we look at each other and tremble with fear that someone will start in again, someone will mutter it between their teeth … And we get in the car as fast as we can and run from the family house.

Rosa. When my uncle from America visited, the whole family gathered together. And the more wine my uncle drank, the farther we traveled. "Tomorrow we'll get up early, get in the car and go to the Tatra Mountains. I'll take care of the hotel."

He didn't get up the next day until lunch.

When Rosa visited him in America, they sat around the table in the evening and made plans about where they'd go the next day. They drank red and traveled to San Francisco, Los Angeles, and New York.

The next day Rosa sat waiting in her room, ready to go.

The house was asleep.

At lunchtime, her uncle got up, brewed himself a big cup of coffee and disappeared behind the newspaper.

Away! Away!

They waited to be rescued. By other places.

All those vacations on the Greek islands: focusing on summer.

Like in that book where the guy on vacation in Italy with a wife he doesn't love realizes he hates his everyday life. His job. Realizes he lives—holds out—only for that month of vacation every year. And he never returns.

But it ends badly anyway.

Son. So, I thought that at the very worst, I'd sit down somewhere in a corner of the Main Station and write something, mark something down.

We weren't born for this, after all.

On the way to work: there's a person crawling on all fours along Commercial Street. It's snowing. Two young people in fatigues are heading toward him. I freeze. They lift him up and sit him down on the window sill of a jewelry shop.

It's November and in front of us is Christmas, the first Christmas without the threat of food!
After I ran away, Son gratefully began to eat what I did. Or what I didn't.

My body was born. Legs are for running. My shoulders relaxed. They shook off their load. The walker became a runner.

Running. A way to deal with loss. Protestsong.

I try not to fixate. Fixate on reindeer.

Oh, let me, let me,
Let me freeze again.

When I flew in from Munich, it was already cold everywhere. But at the airport, vacationers from Hawaii were mixing with the people in their winter coats. I was overwhelmed with pride for the north.

Confused, the summer people were running around the cold baggage that had arrived from Germany. Short-clad folk. Deceived by the south, the exoticism, the warm sea.

A man in a thick sweater and I smiled at each other. We flew in from a country where you have to deserve your warmth, work for it. Set your own fire in your own body. A blaze.

We came from menthol-green rivers, not from the sea.

From springs.

When a person reaches middle-age, everything having to do with the south starts to be suspicious.

We don't have a sea. Nor do we want one...

CHINA (CUPS)

Son's mouth had been through many metamorphoses in a hundred years. Twice he returned from Germany missing the same front tooth. The other one he would pull out on Crete about ten years later, live, under the burning sun, in a restaurant full of people eating lunch. And then right afterward he started pouring handfuls of salted peanuts into his mouth from a bowl in the middle of the table.

Gradually, our mouths stopped fitting together. There was always a gap somewhere from which our common breath could escape.

A draft. A humid stream.

Seemingly overnight we grew something in our mouths and lost something at the same time. Porcelain cups and clumps of candies, the soft insides of a loaf of bread balled up into bits, pieces of Lego. From time to time, we would casually spit one of these into the toilet or, bewildered and cautious, pull it with two fingers out of our mouths and set it on the dessert plate.

We were still lovers then, but something was lost.

Porcelain cups clink against each other. Which one will you drink from?

You know everything about them, and so do your fingers.

Coffee or tea?

Son is smiling at me: almost toothless. I finally have a child.

A little boy, who bubbled up from the pot.

No-body.

The dentist. The problem with those back teeth is that they're removable. But it's not so horrible. You'll get used to it in two weeks.

Son. Hm…It's worse to have a removable leg.

Dentist. What? Hmmmm… Yes, you could say that.

After they pull out his tooth, Son jumps out of the chair in a flash and stands eye-to-eye with the dentist—so quickly that the latter instinctively backs up, as if frightened, as if the patient were confused by the anesthesia and about to attack him. And he would have reason to—the dentist was clenching his still-warm, innocent front tooth in the pliers behind his back.

Too much romance, even for a person in the prime of life.

For a wolf and for a lamb too.

That photograph that won some global competition: Bride and Groom. The groom has no face. It's an American—a soldier who came back from Iraq burned and disfigured. His young wife, a girl, his girlfriend, wanted to keep her promise. A wedding photo in which no one is smiling. How long will it take for the bride to lose her face as well?

The street that leads from the Old Town in Graz to the station. Gradually, the tiny Italian bars, the river, shops full of candy and sweets, disappear. To be replaced by snack bars full of spiced meat and porn shops alternating with wedding rentals and Dutch florists.

Empty. Cold orifices. Leather. Wood. Metal. And repeat. And repeat again. Until the last drop of blood. On the way to pornography and back.

Sometimes a person needs to see their own blood. Under their feet on the steps. On the glass wall. On someone else's skin. Overflowed.

And then. Two faces that begin to radiate at each other.

Roasting one other.

(We are approaching that moment of free play, when the left brain hemisphere relinquishes its power until some formal decision renews its oversight. This structure, so noticeable in music, is typical of many human interactions.)

CHRISTMAS

Christmas at Pierre's. A family party in a restaurant in a mountain valley. Full of air and light. Endless party, endless appetite—so characteristic of a family together. With family, one's gourmandise grows. Family is the scourge of humanity. You look into the faces of your relatives over the table. They push you, further and further. Deeper! You submerge: Into the food! Into the food!
You serve yourself, digging deep into the porcelain/cups.

At Pierre's house we have coffee. He paces around the room, smoking a cigar. The ash falls onto the armchair, the carpet and table. His wife whispers something on the other side of a door with frosted glass: God, Pierre, your ashes are everywhere. As if she were reproaching him for leaking out of a funeral urn.

And she?
Smoke.

People around here always begin to stock up for Christmas in October. While today, it's already clear that one can only live through winter surviving without supplies.

We should eat superficially.

Not cook.

Roast.

Roast in Corman's eyes. Sizzle.

God liked Corman's blue eyes.

And they were the eyes of a charlatan. But maybe you can only roast in the eyes of a charlatan. In clown blue.

The story of bean soup. My story—as a housewife. The day before, as I was about to escape, I still made a full pot of bean soup. Before five in the morning, when I was writing my good-bye note, I realized that after Son read it, he wouldn't want to eat anymore. I thought for a moment about where I could hide the note so that he wouldn't find it until after lunch. So that he wouldn't lose his appetite.

At the bottom of the pot. Into the soup....

Corman had social skills. He knew how to communicate, make arrangements, negotiate, address someone, pay. With strangers. In various languages. He translated for me. He selected food and wine and always made good choices.

Son was always asocial, just like me. And when two asocial people live together, and one of them is a poet and the other a novelist, it's clear that communication with the world will be left to the novelist. Poets are always above it all. Novelists must serve them: arrange things, cook, decorate, put the food on the plate. And then tolerate the frustration that they could never! Never guess what the poet wants!

A woman novelist held captive like this is easily distracted.

A daughter to her mother. Morning in Lapa: Mama, you slept so deeply all night, didn't you? Like a pig.

Son tells me: You see, you said we'd never get out of Lapa. And we're supposed to move in two weeks. And he smiles triumphantly at me. Like I'd gotten out. Like he'd gotten me out.

It's you, you are my Lapa, Son.

In the morning there's a call from John, my American publisher. He's in London. (For years we would work on publishing my book, in the meantime we would become friends, lovers and then friends again and finally we would forget about each other. The book would never come out.) He's depressed. His girlfriend left him. Just now, before Christmas. What the hell is he going to do for the holidays? He had a plan all set: An extraordinarily lavish breakfast, opening gifts, then a walk just the two of them, a celebratory lunch...

John. And now? I'm walking around London by myself, in the city they're already putting up and decorating gigantic Christmas trees. They scare me. This Christmas I'm depressed and terrified.

An American is walking around London terrified of Christmas trees.

And other people? What's terrifying other people around the world at this moment? And what will they fear on Christmas?

I'm afraid that this Christmas won't be how I had imagined it, says John in a serious voice. I'd rather there was no Christmas. No Christmas at all this year.

Thanksgiving Day at the end of November, full stop.

Birthdays, Christmas, New Year's. With Corman there were so many celebrations this autumn. But the dates didn't overlap with the official holidays. A flood of red days on the calendar.

How did it happen with Son? A couple that fits tightly together. They interlock; every part on one body has a corresponding counterpart on the other. A sibling. Everything fits. And then, with time... Something changes, unnoticed. It shifts a little bit. Some spots on the body move. They set off on the road.

Away! Away!

In an embrace, the black holes glom onto each other. Enable each other. Create whole worlds. Black planets. Spinning in the universe between us. Abysses.

The more they fit together, the deeper the hollowness between them. The fuller they were, the hollower they become. EEEEEEchooooo.

Choooobooooooh!

On the road moving from trap to trap. Together, alone again. The echo of his cry follows:

Oh, let me, let me,
Let me again!

CHRISTMAS

On the street, at the Christmas market. Two boys behind me. You know what happened to me the other day? You know what happened to me on Facebook?

Where did I travel? *Whonose*, but I know that in my suitcase I found three pairs of scissors.

Winter. In the store, more and more people make a beeline for the shelves with the cookies. A mix of fat and sugar. Love that warms the belly. Yeast—the quintessence of growth.

There's the season of passion and the season of refined sugar.

CHRISTMAS

During lunch, I went to visit Gergana. To bring her some cookies. She was sitting in a wicker rocking chair. In the middle of an apartment overflowing with dirt. Rocking slowly. We start drinking wine and the sun shines into the room. Merciless light has revived dust bunnies careening like tumbleweeds on the wood floor. They roll and scoot a little sideways. In the draft. I tell her that we should make Bethlehem crèche characters out of those dust bunnies. Like others do with corn husks.

And then back out into a snowy landscape. Big, cold flakes fall into my eyes and onto my lips. Drifts are growing on my shoulders, on my head thrown back, face turned to the sky.

(Without his fine fur coat, Chekhov felt like a vagabond.)

It's Christmas Eve and I have a one-off waitressing job. I'm going to City Hall—year after year the mayor's wife serves Christmas dinner here to those who are alone. In her speech, she says that she would be happy if many more people could fit into the hall and at the same time if there weren't anyone there at all. The lonely ones.

The lonely ones peer at each other curiously. They size each other up, comparing their relative level of loneliness. Whether they really deserve this invitation to City Hall. Who chose them? The lonely ones. And according to what criteria? How did they actually come up with this mix?

Then, Christmas at home. Son, Chilean wine, walnuts, Christmas cookies, mistletoe… A full table of food & symbols & traditions, until your stomach turns. Metamorphosis of passion.

Your muteness means always…(just a bit) satiating with silent lamb

And then. Finally, dinner at the parents' house as well. Mama looks at me quizzically. Have you been drinking already? Daughter of mine…

Whonose.

Yes, Mama. The whole time. Everywhere.

Rosa. What's left? A little bit of gold dust remains on the tips of the fingers. On the hem of the pants.

Son wrote in his diary—24, 25, 26 December: nothing, nothing, nothing.

NEW YEAR'S

Rosa. A midnight conversation with Son. About Kerouac and Ginsberg. On a nighttime walk through Lapa. Belly full of wine. Anesthesia.

I'm saying that I am, unfortunately, much more like Kerouac than Ginsberg. After midnight, I wake up to Son looking at me in bed. I had told him that early in the morning I'd be going to Vienna. With Gergana. It seems suspicious to him, that I should go so early in the morning. He'll never forget how I ran away. He'll never forgive me. Nor himself, for not waking up at five. Fully armed!

He tells me that he doesn't understand.

— What don't you understand?
— I just don't understand…
— But, for God's sake, what?…
— Why are you more like Kerouac than Ginsberg?

Because Kerouac was a hysteric. Falling apart. Sweet wines, port in the morning, chaotic, climbing hills that other men had lauded, but even on the way up he looked forward to the day he would come down again. Back to messy towns. He couldn't stand solitude, tranquility, nature. He feared elemental sounds— wind, rain, rustling trees, air, animals. But he was always seeking them out.

Messed up city bitch!

Like me! Like me! I drank too much wine again yesterday.

A full stomach—slosh-slosh-slosh-shoop.

(no recovery allowed)

A good nighttime discussion. The only ones missing in the bed were Corso and Ferlinghetti.

Son and I are sitting at lunch, smoking Corman's cigarettes.

On the terrace, a young man says into his cell phone: So, like, where were you, you cunt? All night?

NEW YEAR'S

On New Year's two piles of walnut shells reached toward the ceiling. Nutshells and the shells of cracked peanuts. They gobbled them at night, pressed them to the roofs of their mouths, put them under their tongues, washed them down with wine. In a vulnerable conversation interlaced with powerful silence. A combination of various kinds of quiet.

Two piles of shells at opposite ends of the table. Like the result of a passion that erupted in the household of two raging old squirrels.

NORA

Rosa. Illness. The doctor tells me. Madam, I need your urine!

A bad sign. In Paris, one night: I bought a bottle of sauvignon blanc and after the third glass I knocked over the balsamic vinegar. The thick, dark brown liquid splashed onto the kitchen window and ran down the wall behind the radiator. Luckily, the bottle didn't break, nor did all of it spill out. A good sign?

Not only the crumbs on the table belong to the god Pan. We're always buying him something, chasing something down, indulging him. Cigarettes, alcohol, coffee, books, treats, clothing, cars, apartments, houses, countries, planets.

This morning the second light bulb in the hallway went out. The light is receding.

Gergana tells me she had a bad day. She was at the playground with her son and they saw a little girl there who looked like an angel. But when the boy wanted to play with her, she pushed him away saying that she wasn't going to play with him because she was pulling beer on tap. What a bitch-child. Gergana says. With her strong accent. "So we went to another playground. There we met a little boy who threw my son's ball into the prickly bushes on purpose. Another bitch-child."
Changing playgrounds doesn't solve anything.

Nor countrics.

When did it actually begin to end? When a woman, on a walk through the city, by chance spies the back or the profile of her man in the distance. And instead of running after him (as she would have even yesterday), surprised by this sudden image of her love, she stops and waits until his figure recedes into the distance and gradually disappears.

And for the rest of her walk she wonders whether he would have been capable of the same.

Whether he too is such a fake, lying, cheating prick, another bitch-child.

I leaf through the telephone book, jumping from name to name. Seriously? I don't have one friend? A girlfriend? No one I can meet up with? Just to talk? Name after name.
(Every person is a plot, Corman claimed.)
In the end, you stay home alone, proudly watching the label on a bottle.

Son says, Slovak late harvest wine—sour, but strong.

In it you taste tones of blackberry and old rags.

Sunday terror. Wherever I go, chicken-noodle soup breathes down my neck.

Son tries hard to hug me, to take me in his arms. How helpless he is when I avoid him. I move out of the way. How he says: Please, just for a minute, just give me a minute. But I, I can't give anymore. I can't be sealed in. Like a child pushed away by its parents, he doesn't get it. Women never left Son. Only Mama. His mother died on him. And now I, in his eyes, am senselessly, needlessly and cruelly on strike. Like some entitled Parisian students.

And he tries to get me in his arms again. To carry? Mostly to be carried. But how can you carry a 100-kilo child through the world? A 100-kilo child with a beard and mustache, with a tear in one eye and oil in the other. Anger in place of eyebrows.

I'm running, past an old tree. With a big tire stuck in its hollow. A secret?

Benjamin writes that if you never run away from home when you're 16, you miss out on a formative experience, one important for the rest of your life. Even if it only lasts 48 hours. You'll never have another chance, won't be able to catch up.

It's just as important to run away from your man when you're 30.

And then you find yourself nursing a cup of tea in some room. And you recall all the women you sneered at when you were a twenty something. (Nora & Co.)

The last antibiotics this morning, and the feeling that maybe, finally, HEALTH! "Very soon—money and love," added Fernando Pessoa, at 30, to his horoscope.

Yeah? So did any of it come true for him? asks Son. Only the "very" part.

AFTER THE NEW (YEAR)

Son is testing me. He looks at me, frowning. Like a bodhisattva. I exercise. He glares.

A couple of times, in between individual exercises in the series, I pounce on him. I hug his motionlessness. He stays still.

The master.

When, after all of that, he finally opens his arms, I can't anymore. I push him away.

Five Tibetans, two Slovaks.

I stand in the doorway, I'm trussed, I call, instead of dressed.

The reindeer and horse disappeared. Once in a while I still hear the clip-clop of hooves in my sleep.

Imagine that you're a little girl, whose entire / colorful little childhood . changes without you noticing into / an enormous bus station full of quiet / sleeping, air-conditioned monsters.

It's evening. We are each in a different corner of the room. At our own tables. Quietly writing, our backs turned to each other. Quietly writing. Recording all that anger, the tears and helplessness. We each heap all of it on the other in our Moleskin—Soreskin notebooks. Like two lunatics. Pathetic souls. Dummies. Writers.

THE KING

On this street I am king, you say, after we've moved onto the Hill.

Your words, spouted, whispered, babbled, heightening the voice / futile, futile, futile / your words, king, encircling / airtight / liberating, shoreless, clamping / laying supine / pulsing / vibrating and lashing / the air in our apartment and blood in veins / distending our summer quilt. Your words / turn out of home and send on the road back / prowl / stalk / Your words / king / open bottles / on the jambs of blown-away doors / shoot century-old corks / fling windows wide and push children / as if by the bye / towards the nearest cliff / Your words / my images / Your words /my country / native land / flag / Your words / the only possible social order / Your words / chocolate with lumps of crystallised earth / fairtrade / Your words / trophies / of my stopped-up rifle / Your words / enthusiastically / pitch my body to the sky / like an empty / summer ball.

Stripey and flowery / to death.

Was that life? May it come again!

And in the new apartment, where unpacked bags of books stand like an army. Instead of being filled with flour, sugar and salt. You fly like some new-born predator, reduced to bones and the embryonic smile of a skinny animal. A tapir with a long snout that can run along the bottom of the sea.

An animal, with whom it would be possible *again*.

Again, maybe in spite of my own wooden body. If only this weren't hanging in the air:

Hmmmm, odd, I've never lived with a statue before.

Can I at least look?

Son and Rosa. In the woods. It's quiet; they hear only their own footsteps. *Grrrrr,* Rosa suddenly hears right behind her. She freezes. A wolf. It's quiet again for a minute. She must have imagined it. *Grrrr,* again right above her head—she looks around and sees nothing.

But in her backpack her cell phone is vibrating. Like a wild animal. Always at her heels.
Her own toes hopping happily on her back.

A strange ballet.

We are swathed in a new landscape. That view! as my mother used to say, when we would stand on a hill as kids. You see that view, kids? Drink it in.

And what's more: those new, quiet rooms with the ceilings just below the sky. And a bed.

I bought a bed! wrote Rosa proudly to John. And he wrote back that he himself has bought many beds in his life. But that the actual act of purchasing never excited him as much as that.

(Naturally, not as much as her, the materialistic Slovak woman!) Who, for the first time at the age of 36, has enough money scraped together that she can simply go and buy a double bed. Both halves at once.

Rich? Oh, let me / let me again.

Because, as Pessoa once wrote full of hope: Very soon—money & love.

And shortly after that he died. He kicked the bucket in the hospital. *Grrrrr,* sang his own liver to him under the down quilt.

Glossed up with cheap alcohol—sour cherries carried away & submerged in red liquor.

In the country where he lived, they sell it in small dark rooms and people take it out in front of the stands, onto the streets and squares. And they swirl those cherries in glasses, swirl them, right under the midday sun.

Again and again. It purrs on the crowns of their heads.

Grrrgrrrr: radiates.

— Yes, I know it, you already told me about that.

— Yeah, I know, I do remember that I already told you. I talk about it constantly. I'm polishing it.

Stories that I listened to so breathlessly at the beginning— ground down by the years.

Grrrrrgrrrrr.
Stories that you refine.

You sand & burnish, level off & polish alternately against my forehead and crown.

In the tram you turn to me and start. There's no escape, in vain I demonstratively turn my whole body away from you toward the window. You refine, hone, strive to constantly pump something into me. Best if it's directly into my ear, straight to the face. You command full attention. When I ask you to stop talking to me, for God's sake, stop! stop!—the only thing you do is talk faster.

What to do? Where to hide?

Away! Away!

Kingson, you are my heavy metal.

And I think of that woman who was once sitting behind me on the tram. Small, round, middle-aged. Every time the car started up from a stop, she pounded on the window with her fist.

(*Whonose* what she was refining.)

I'm getting closer to it. To the point of pounding with my fist.

Grrrrrrgrrrrgrrrr.

Silence.

Behind me sit young lovers, slim & suntanned:
You know, I was thinking about it, that if it happened to me, to my own mother, I probably wouldn't be able to deal with it. I would rather put her in a facility. I'm too sensitive to watch my own mother pee on herself. That wouldn't be my thing.

The Hill is beautiful. Whenever I think that I'll run away from the king someday, I already regret in advance that I would lose this view, this panorama. Everything would be swallowed up by the Earth. The landscape you brought me to.

Your muteness means always...(just a bit) satiating with silent lamb

On the road below the wood I meet a shepherd with his goats.
He talks to me:
And what are you doing here? Visiting someone?
No, I actually just moved here.

In that case, welcome. We'll stay in touch.

And a couple of short flashes follow, and you tell me that you know what it's like. That story of how you can fall ill from being with someone who talks incessantly. How one can exasperate the other with speech. And you begin with this story of how a woman used to come to your house and she talked too much and your mother always became unwell after she left. Your mother developed a migraine, her head hurt, she would feel faint & vomit. And as you're honing that story, my head begins to hurt and I throw up breakfast. That's how the world ends. With long & complicated talk about a migraine from which fresh nausea sprouts.

In the migraine chain.

Son. Everything just degrades and degrades. People just recycle the same six words.

It doesn't matter, says Rosa, the end of the world is coming anyway.

Son. The end of the world? Oh come ooooon! That'll just be another hot topic and then nothing will happen and we'll all go on like before...

We'll stay in touch.

Some stories so need telling, that one is forced to constantly look for new listeners—friends, lovers, so that one can tell them repeatedly and from the beginning. With all the details, as if they were completely new. Born again.

Communists and capitalists—those are the main characters of some of Son's morning programs.

That polished-to-gold story about two poets who meet in the Tatra Mountains on New Year's, one from communist Czechoslovakia, the other from West Germany. And the first one says: Ah, one more day that we've managed to steal from the communists.

And the one from Germany responds: Ah, one more day that we've managed to steal from the capitalists.

In the distance, I hear the clip-clop of hooves. A horse and rider or the devil? I put one ear to the ground, and then the other.

A dream. Into a restaurant where Son and I are having dinner bursts an armed commando. We are taken into some far away back room. I'm afraid and talking constantly. In the room, a row of killers sit at a long judge's table. Each one has a card in his hand. After a while I see that on each one it says: ROSA.

(Son. Death to the occupiers! Ice cream to us!)

The king descends upon the shelf full of bottles. He plunges his hand into them and the bottles fall like dominoes. I feel like it will never end—the falling, splashing, shattering, broken bottle necks. Then silence. Squelching of wine and clinking of shards in sandals.

And so begins the final drama.

Let me go, please, I say to the king.

Your muteness means always…(just a bit) satiating with silent lamb.

He says he doesn't know what I'm talking about. He says.

And his body begins to run wild by itself. He senses that his luck is running out.

Grrrrgrrrr.

From his original body, the only things left are two beautiful legs with defined ropes of muscle. As hard as well-braided hair. Hanging down from the waist. Two reminders of a body.

Powerful and lithe at the same time, he had the body of a swimmer with broad shoulders. His chest rounded and hot like the sun. With a narrow trunk and no hips.

He changes from one day to the next, gaining weight, expanding and suffering, expanding and suffering—a Slovak Marlon Brando.

He inflates, full of air like a water toy in summer. He swims around the apartment. Trying to block all the emergency exits. Filling the space.

Excruciating. A scene so sad one could burst. Cracking apart.

The body I've loved for years closes me in like a prison. It has plugged the exits, blocked the road. All those folds piled up in the doorway. He always lies so that I can't get out of bed without climbing. He overflows from my side of the bed to the door. Grows like a hill in spring. Trying to prevent any sort of uncontrolled movement. A living barricade. Seeded lightly from above. With wild poppies. A dam-ossuary. Flowing over the edge with sharp elbows and round knees.

Your arm makes a right angle to your body. An arch above my head. *Enclosure without embrace.*

Rosa's day begins with the struggle of how to get out of bed. To go beyond the city walls. Climb over the fort, swim across the moat. The king holds on, eyes closed. Feigning sleep. Electricity in the dog-collar ready. And when she thinks she's made it and cleared the bar, he opens his eyes and asks with a smile: Where are you going? Where to?

JANA BEŇOVÁ is one of the most acclaimed Slovak writers, and winner of the European Union Prize for Literature. She is a poet and novelist, author of the novels *Seeing People Off*, *Parker*, and *Honeymoon*, as well as three collections of poems.

JANET LIVINGSTONE was born in Boston, Massachusetts, and ventured to Czechoslovakia just after the 1989 Velvet Revolution. Bratislava, Slovakia, was her home for over 15 years. In 2003, she began translating films and plays from Slovak to English and hasn't looked back since. Among her full-length book translations are *Seeing People Off* by Jana Beňová and *Piata loď* (working title: *Boat Number Five*) by novelist Monika Kompaníková. Her current translation projects include the novels *The Best of All Worlds* by Slovak-Swiss author Irena Brežná and *The Arab World—Another Planet?* by Emire Khidayer. Janet lives in Seattle and also speaks French, Italian, Russian, Spanish and elementary Japanese to anyone who will listen.

NOTE FROM THE AUTHORS

The poem titled "The King," which appears in this book, was translated by Irish poet and translator John Minahane.

The author and translator would like to thank editor Terezia Cicel for the fruitful collaboration.

Two Dollar Radio
Books too loud to Ignore

ALSO AVAILABLE Here are some other titles you might want to dig into.

SEEING PEOPLE OFF NOVEL BY JANA BEŇOVÁ
TRANSLATED BY JANET LIVINGSTONE

→ **Winner of the European Union Prize for Literature**

← "A fascinating novel. Fans of inward-looking post-modernists like Clarice Lispector will find much to admire." —NPR

A KALEIDOSCOPIC, POETIC, AND DARKLY FUNNY portrait of a young couple navigating post-socialist Slovakia.

THE DEEPER THE WATER THE UGLIER THE FISH NOVEL BY KATYA APEKINA

← "Brilliantly structured... refreshingly original, and the writing is nothing short of gorgeous. It's a stunningly accomplished book." —NPR

POWERFULLY CAPTURES THE QUIET TORMENT of two sisters craving the attention of a parent they can't, and shouldn't, have to themselves.

THE BLURRY YEARS NOVEL BY ELEANOR KRISEMAN

← "Kriseman's is a new voice to celebrate." —*Publishers Weekly*

THE BLURRY YEARS IS A POWERFUL and unorthodox coming-of-age story from an assured new literary voice, featuring a stirringly twisted mother-daughter relationship, set against the sleazy, vividly-drawn backdrop of late-seventies and early-eighties Florida.

THE UNDERNEATH NOVEL BY MELANIE FINN

← "*The Underneath* is an excellent thriller." —*Star Tribune*

THE UNDERNEATH IS AN INTELLIGENT and considerate exploration of violence—both personal and social—and whether violence may ever be justified. With the assurance and grace of her acclaimed novel *The Gloaming*, Melanie Finn returns with a precisely layered and tense new literary thriller.

Thank you for supporting independent culture!
Feel good about yourself.

Books to read!

THE GLOAMING NOVEL BY **MELANIE FINN**

→ **New York Times Notable Book of 2016**

← "Deeply satisfying." —*New York Times Book Review*

AFTER AN ACCIDENT LEAVES her estranged in a Swiss town, Pilgrim Jones absconds to east Africa, settling in a Tanzanian outpost where she can't shake the unsettling feeling that she's being followed.

WHITE DIALOGUES STORIES **BENNETT SIMS**

← "Anyone who admires such pyrotechnics of language will find 21st-century echoes of Edgar Allan Poe in Sims' portraits of paranoia and delusion, with their zodiacal narrowing and the maddening tungsten spin of their narratives." —*New York Times Book Review*

IN THESE ELEVEN STORIES, Sims moves from slow-burn psychological horror to playful comedy, bringing us into the minds of people who are haunted by their environments, obsessions, and doubts.

THE ONLY ONES NOVEL BY **CAROLA DIBBELL**

→ **Best Books 2015:** *Washington Post*; *O, The Oprah Magazine*; NPR

← "Breathtaking." —NPR

INEZ WANDERS A POST-PANDEMIC world immune to disease. Her life is altered when a grief-stricken mother that hired her to provide genetic material backs out, leaving Inez with the product: a baby girl.

FOUND AUDIO NOVEL BY **N.J. CAMPBELL**

← "[A] mysterious work of metafiction… dizzying, arresting and defiantly bold." —*Chicago Tribune*

← "This strange little book, full of momentum, intrigue, and weighty ideas to mull over, is a bona fide literary page-turner." —*Publishers Weekly*, "Best Summer Books, 2017"

THE VINE THAT ATE THE SOUTH
NOVEL BY **J.D. WILKES**

← "Undeniably one of the smartest, most original Southern Gothic novels to come along in years." —NPR

WITH THE ENERGY AND UNIQUE VISION that established him as a celebrated musician, Wilkes here is an accomplished storyteller on a Homeric voyage that strikes at the heart of American mythology.

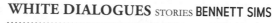

Books to read!

THEY CAN'T KILL US UNTIL THEY KILL US ESSAYS BY **HANIF ABDURRAQIB**

→ **Best Books 2017**: NPR, *Buzzfeed, Paste Magazine, Esquire, Chicago Tribune, Vol. 1 Brooklyn,* CBC (Canada), *Stereogum, National Post* (Canada), *Entropy, Heavy, Book Riot, Chicago Review of Books* (November), *The Los Angeles Review, Michigan Daily*

← "Funny, painful, precise, desperate, and loving throughout. Not a day has sounded the same since I read him."
—Greil Marcus, *Village Voice*

PALACES NOVEL BY **SIMON JACOBS**

← "*Palaces* is robust, both current and clairvoyant… With a pitch-perfect portrayal of the punk scene and idiosyncratic, meaty characters, this is a wonderful novel that takes no prisoners." —*Foreword Reviews,* starred review

WITH INCISIVE PRECISION and a cool detachment, Simon Jacobs has crafted a surreal and spellbinding first novel of horror and intrigue.

NOT DARK YET NOVEL BY **BERIT ELLINGSEN**

← "Fascinating, surreal, gorgeously written."
—*BuzzFeed*

ON THE VERGE OF a self-inflicted apocalypse, a former military sniper is enlisted by a former lover for an eco-terrorist action that threatens the quiet life he built for himself in the mountains.

THE REACTIVE NOVEL BY **MASANDE NTSHANGA**

← "Often teems with a beauty that seems to carry on in front of its glue-huffing wasters despite themselves." —*Slate*

A CLEAR-EYED, COMPASSIONATE ACCOUNT of a young HIV+ man grappling with the sudden death of his brother in South Africa.

THE INCANTATIONS OF DANIEL JOHNSTON
GRAPHIC NOVEL BY **RICARDO CAVOLO**
WRITTEN BY **SCOTT MCCLANAHAN**

← "Wholly unexpected, grotesque, and poignant." —*The FADER*

RENOWNED ARTIST RICARDO CAVOLO and Scott McClanahan combine talents in this dazzling, eye-popping graphic biography of artist and musician Daniel Johnston.